AF584962

With thanks to

Melbourne Maritime Heritage Network

Geoffrey Evans Trust

English Speaking Union Victoria

Offshore and Specialist Ships Australia

PICTURE CREDITS: I
llustrations on pages 8, 9, 10 and 36
are by Tommy McCrae from
Book of Sketches of Aboriginal Life.
Pen and Ink Drawings by 19th Century
Aboriginal Australian artist,
Tommy McCrae (1836 – 1901 approx).
State Library of Victoria

To all the young mariners past and present. C.W.

To Graham. P.P.

To the rivers and bay that have sustained the people of Melbourne for 60,000 years. M.M.H.M.

First published in 2023 by
wild dog
Melbourne, Australia
wdog.com.au

ISBN: 9781742036168

A catalogue record for this book is available from the National Library of Australia

10 9 8 7 6 5 4 3 2 1   23 24 25 26 27

Printed and bound in China by
Everbest Printing Investment Limited

FSC® is a non-profit international organisation established to promote the responsible management of the world's forests.

River to Bay

Victoria's Maritime History

CAROLE WILKINSON & PRUE PITTOCK

Contents

Melbourne / Naarm
Fishermans Bend
Williamstown
Yarra River / Birrarung
Sandridge / Port Melbourne
Hobsons Bay
ort Gellibrand
Port Phillip
South Channel Fort
Point Nepean
Fort Pearce
Point King
Sorrento /
Sullivan Bay
Settlement Site
Western Port
French Island
ornington Peninsula
Phillip Island

First Peoples

Aboriginal people had lived on the Victorian coast and on the banks of the Birrarung for more than 60,000 years before Europeans came.

The Woiwurrung people of the Kulin Nation lived on the banks of the river, the creeks, swamps and billabongs that fed into it. The Boonwurrung people, where it emptied into the bay they called Nerm or Nairm. The coastline, the river and its banks provided food for the Kulin. Often, women collected shellfish, plants and reptiles, while men hunted kangaroos and set traps for eels.

At one spot along the river, a row of boulders created a shallow waterfall. Fresh water flowed above the falls. Salt water flowed below. All five clans of the Kulin Nation met there to trade, arrange marriages and hold ceremonies. In the evenings, after their business was finished, they celebrated.

When the Kulin first saw tall ships in the bay and white people rowing up the Birrarung, they didn't realise their Country was about to be invaded. The waterways that were vital as meeting places and as a source of food and fresh water would also be important to the Europeans. These waterways became the sites of the first European settlements in Victoria.

1802

In January 1802, the governor of New South Wales, Governor King, sent the ship *Lady Nelson* to explore the south coast. It was a small ship commanded by John Murray. When the *Lady Nelson* reached the narrow entrance to a bay, Murray was cautious, but he finally sailed into the bay on 14 February and went ashore with some of his crew. At a place he named Bowen Point, near present-day Sorrento, they met local Boonwurrung people and offered them gifts of bread, mirrors and tomahawks. The ship's boy noticed a group of Boonwurrung men holding spears, as if ready to throw. He called out a warning.

Fatal Experience...

The Boonwurrung men launched their spears. None of Murray's men were injured. A crew member fired a warning shot over the heads of the Boonwurrung. They weren't frightened. Murray decided to teach them a lesson 'by fatal experience'. The Europeans shot several Aboriginal men. Once back on board the *Lady Nelson*, Murray ordered his crew to fire the ship's cannon at the men on shore.

and an Invitation to Lunch

In March, Murray raised the British flag on Point King, taking possession of the bay in the name of King George III. Murray named the bay Port Phillip after the first governor of New South Wales.

About ten weeks later, after a long journey from England on the *Investigator*, Matthew Flinders sailed into Port Phillip. At first, he thought he had arrived at Western Port, which had already been explored by his friend George Bass. However, Flinders soon realised he'd reached a different bay.

Although the *Investigator* was far larger than the *Lady Nelson*, Flinders was less cautious than Murray.

Flinders sailed confidently through the narrow entrance, only to run aground on a mud bank. Once the crew freed the ship, Flinders explored the bay. He was surprised that such a small entrance led to a bay that was big enough to anchor 'a larger fleet of ships than ever yet went to sea'.

While exploring Port Phillip, Flinders also encountered Kulin men. He gave them gifts, but instead of shooting at them, he offered to share his lunch of roast duck.

A Gardener's Journal

In Sydney, Governor King heard about Port Phillip and thought it might be a good place for another penal colony. He sent Acting Surveyor, General Charles Grimes, on the *Cumberland* to survey the bay. Grimes was to report on the suitability of the bay area for farming and as a location for a penal colony.

The crew that sailed with Grimes included a convict named James Flemming. He had been transported to New South Wales for seven years for stealing clover seeds. In Sydney, he had a reputation for being a good gardener.
He was included in the survey party to provide his opinion on whether the soil was good enough to grow crops.

This party found what Murray and Flinders had failed to find – the mouth of a large freshwater river – the Birrarung. They rowed up the river. When the river split in two, they continued on the right branch until a waterfall prevented them going further.

1803

Flemming, however, kept a detailed journal that became the official record of the exploration. The gardener was more enthusiastic about the land – especially the site near the falls. He thought it would provide excellent pasture and be a good location for a settlement.

Grimes drew an accurate map of the bay, but kept only brief notes. He was not impressed by Port Phillip, claiming the soil was 'bad' and 'stony', with few trees and a great deal of 'swampy' land.

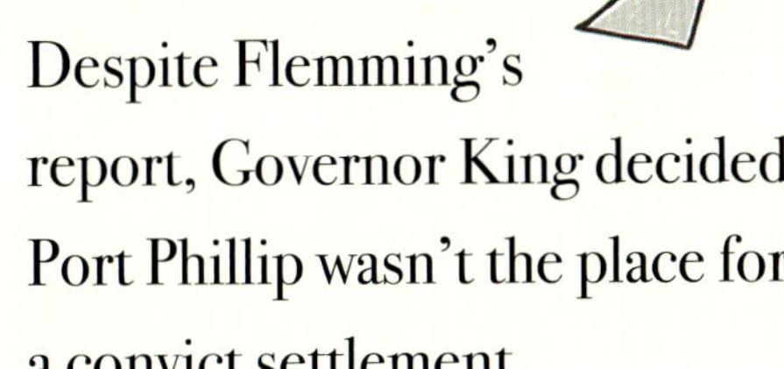

Despite Flemming's report, Governor King decided Port Phillip wasn't the place for a convict settlement.

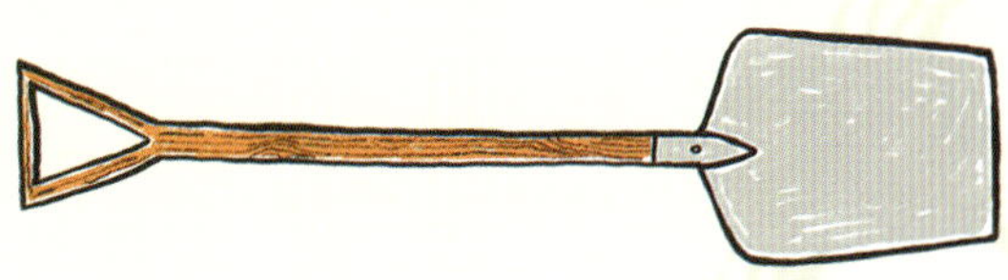

What King didn't know was that the British Government had already decided to establish a convict settlement at Port Phillip. More than 300 convicts were on their way.

Sullivan Bay Settlement

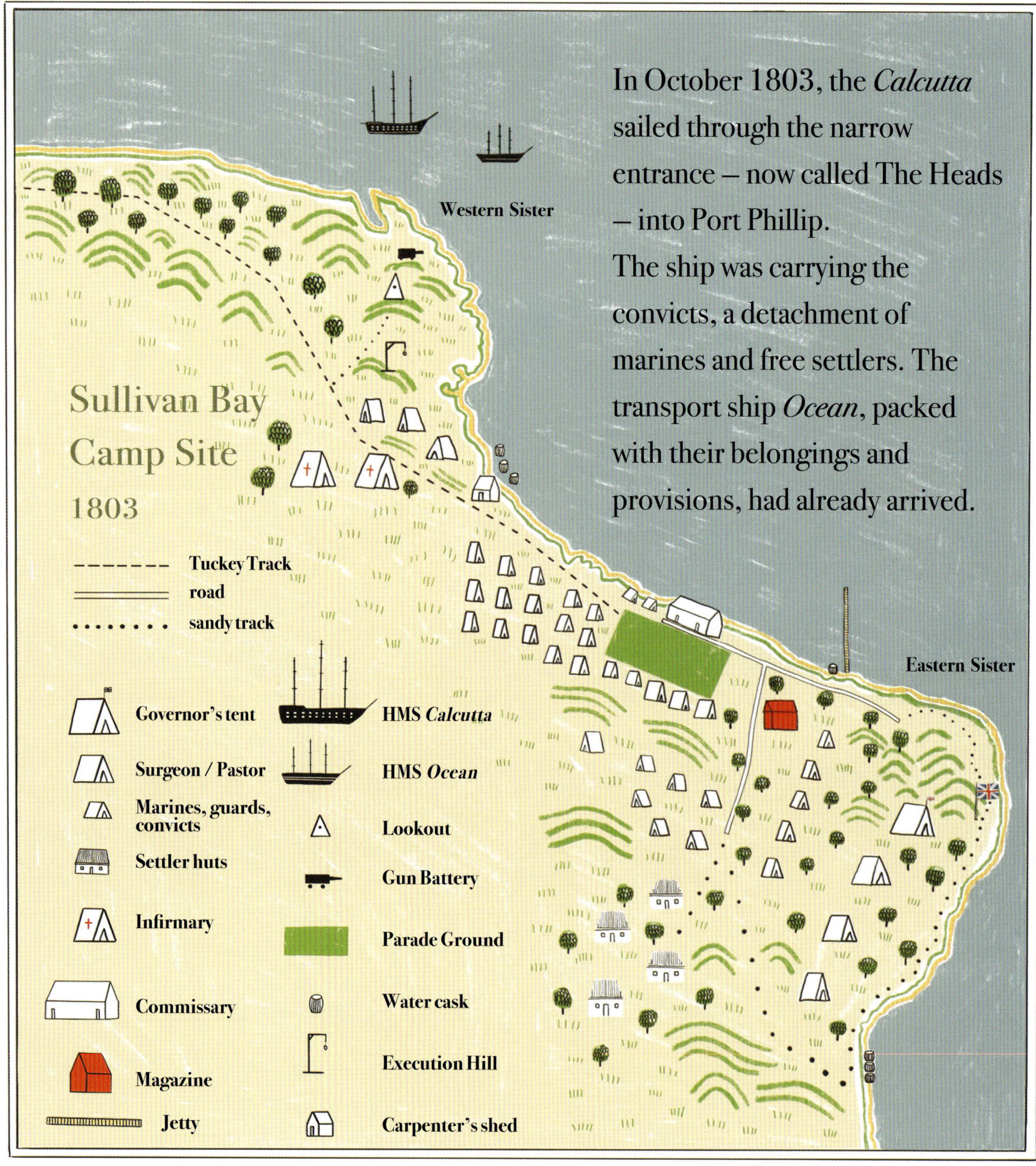

Settlement commander, Lieutenant Governor David Collins, set up camp in a sheltered bay, a few kilometres east of The Heads. Collins named it Sullivan Bay. There was no fresh water and few trees to provide timber for building. The sandy soil was unsuitable for growing wheat.

1803–1804

Collins sent a party of men to look for fresh water. During their unsuccessful search the Europeans met a group of Kulin men armed with spears. The marine in charge ordered his men to shoot. One Kulin man was killed.

Without fresh water, the newcomers had to come up with a way to filter sea water. They drilled holes in barrels and buried them on the beach. This allowed sea water to wash through and leave behind still salty but drinkable water.

Everyone lived in tents. Along with the salted meat they had brought with them, they ate shellfish, ducks and parrots.

They had no success hunting kangaroos.

When news arrived from Sydney that Britain was at war with France, most of the marines left to join the war. This left the convicts unguarded and the settlers undefended.

Collins wrote to the governor saying that Port Phillip was unsuitable for a penal colony. He wanted to move the group to Van Diemen's Land. The governor gave his permission. After seven months at Sullivan Bay, the settlers sailed to the south coast of Van Diemen's Land.

If they had stayed at Port Phillip, the settlement might have grown into the capital of Victoria. Instead, the Sullivan Bay group helped establish Hobart. After the Europeans left, the Kulin population of Port Phillip had 30 years of peace before the next white settlers arrived.

Batman and Fawkner

Two men are linked to creating the first permanent European settlement on Port Phillip. Neither had government permission to do so. Both men were sons of convicts, lived in Van Diemen's Land and wanted to make their fortune.

John Pascoe Fawkner was born in London and came to Australia with his convict father on the *Calcutta*. Fawkner and his family were among the Sullivan Bay settlers who moved to Van Diemen's Land. Fawkner was ten-years-old at the time.

Throughout his life, Fawkner was often in trouble with the law. He planned to sail to Port Phillip in 1835, but he was not allowed to leave Van Diemen's Land until

1835

he had paid his debts. When his ship, the *Enterprize*, arrived at Port Phillip in May 1835, Fawkner was not on board.

John Batman was born in Parramatta. His father, mother, and wife were all convicts, but he was a free man. When he was 21-years-old, Batman moved to Van Diemen's Land, where he was involved in the Black War to remove all Aboriginal people from Tasmania.

Batman and other men from Van Diemen's Land formed the Port Phillip Association. Their goal was to take up prime farming land around the bay. Batman arrived on the *Rebecca* three days after Fawkner's people. He declared the grassy land perfect for grazing sheep. Unlike the Sullivan Bay settlers, Batman located the all-important source of fresh water – the Birrarung. Near the falls, he wrote in his journal his famous statement 'This will be the place for a village'. One of the men accompanying Batman asked the Wurundjeri people the name of the river. When they replied 'Yarro-yarro', meaning 'flowing', he thought they said 'Yarra Yarra'. The name was soon shortened to Yarra River.

Batman had with him an important document. It was a treaty drawn up by a lawyer in Van Diemen's Land. He was ready to make a deal.

Treaty 1835

On 6 June 1835, John Batman met with eight Wurundjeri Elders. He wrote that the three main chiefs, as he called them, were brothers. They were all over 6 feet tall and had the same name. He explained to the Elders that he wanted to buy their land. According to his journal, the Elders agreed to sell 500,000 acres in exchange for blankets, knives, mirrors, tomahawks, beads, scissors and flour.

Batman presented the parchment document he had brought from Van Diemen's Land. According to his journal, all eight Elders signed the treaty. The Wurundjeri Elders, however, could not speak English, and the Aboriginal men who Batman had brought with him from Sydney did not understand Woiwurrung.

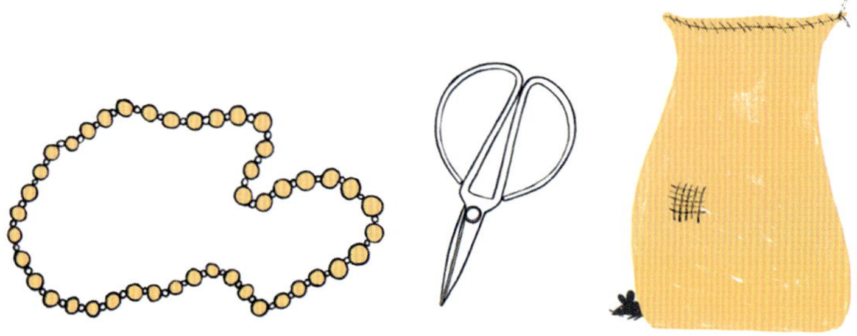

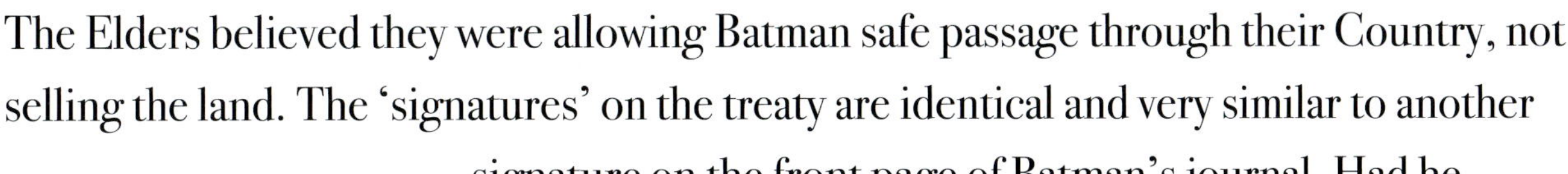

The Elders believed they were allowing Batman safe passage through their Country, not selling the land. The 'signatures' on the treaty are identical and very similar to another signature on the front page of Batman's journal. Had he practised writing it and signed the treaty himself on behalf of the Elders? Afterwards, Batman claimed he was 'the greatest landowner in the world'.

A few months later, Governor Bourke declared that Batman's treaty was illegal.

Fawkner arrived in Port Phillip in October 1835 and claimed he was the founder of the settlement. He was not the first to arrive, but he published its first newspaper, opened its first hotel, and later became a member of its first parliament.

1836–1841

One year after Batman and Fawkner staked their claims on the settlement, almost 200 Europeans and 3000 sheep were living there.

There were just thirteen permanent buildings, including Fawkner's inn, a blacksmith's shop, wooden houses and mud huts. Most settlers lived in tents.

Settlers continued to arrive from Sydney and Hobart. The ships carrying them tied-up to ti-tree poles in the river. Cargo was unloaded onto the riverbank.

As the township grew, debate over its name began. Batman had called it Batmania. Fawkner wanted to name it Glenelg, after Lord Glenelg in England. It was briefly called Bearbrass, which may have been a mispronunciation of Birrarung.

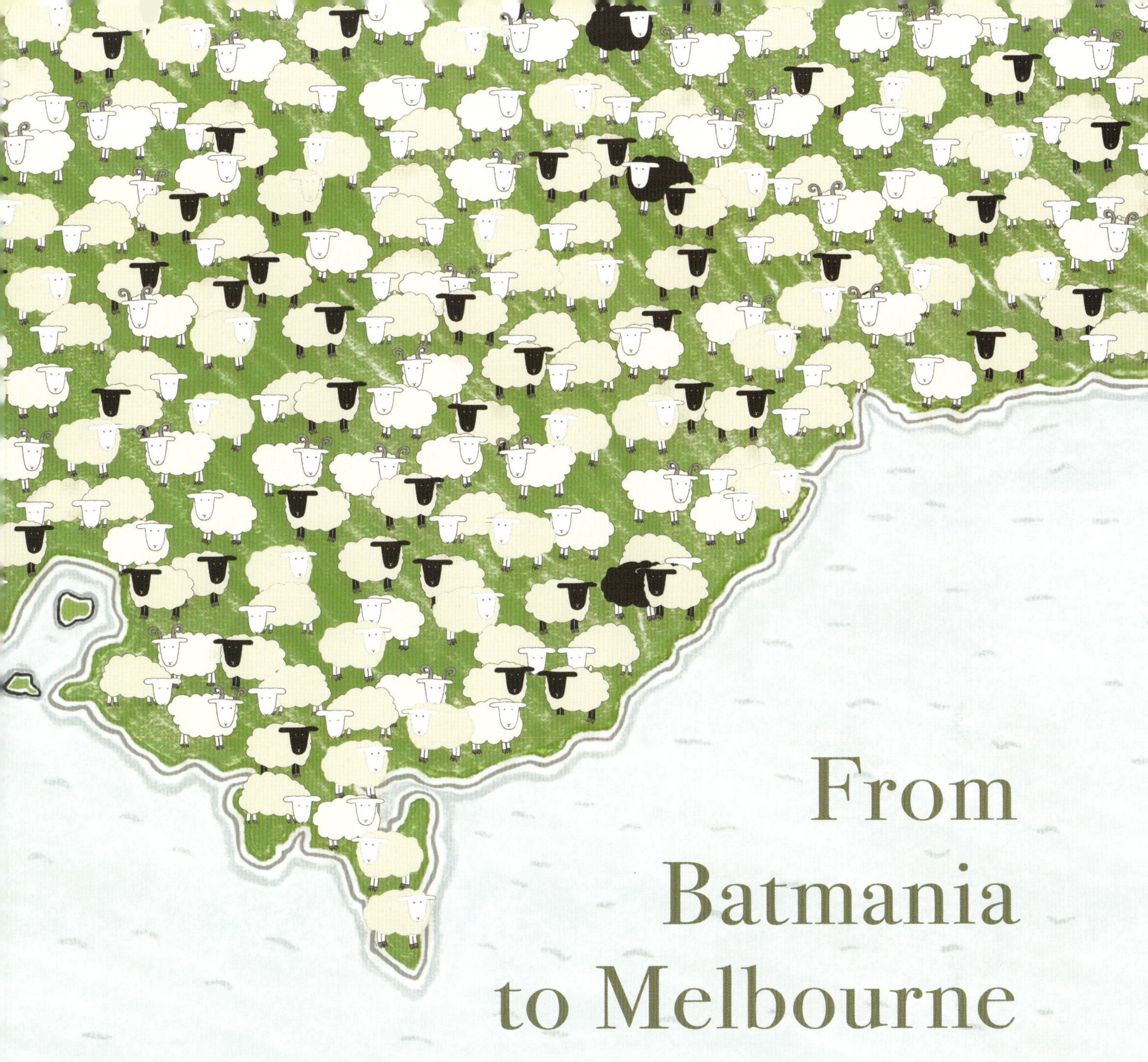

From Batmania to Melbourne

When Governor Bourke visited in 1837, he decided the town needed a more dignified name. He called it Melbourne after British Prime Minister, William Lamb, 2nd Viscount Melbourne.

Surveyor, Robert Hoddle, laid out a plan for the township. It was a simple rectangle bounded by Flinders Street, La Trobe Street, Spencer Street and Spring Street. The land between was divided into 32 ten acre blocks.

With so many ships arriving, Melbourne needed wharves where passengers could disembark and cargo could be unloaded. The first wharf was built by George Ward Cole in 1841 alongside Flinders Street. Other wharves followed. Soon the riverbank was bristling with ships' masts.

Fever Ships 1839–1852

Early ships always carried small, unwelcome stowaways – fleas, lice, cockroaches and rats – which were annoying for the passengers. However, some stowaways were more than annoying. They were deadly. A microscopic bacteria called *Salmonella typhi* infected passengers with the lethal disease typhoid. It spread quickly in overcrowded ships. Vessels carrying passengers with typhoid were called 'fever ships'.

The first fever ship to arrive in Port Phillip was the *Glen Huntly* in 1840. Fifty of its 157 passengers were infected with typhoid. Ten of them died at sea. More died after the ship anchored.

In 1852, the British Government chartered American clipper ship the *Ticonderoga* to transport migrants from England to Australia. Even though it was one of the larger, roomier ships, it turned out to be Australia's worst fever ship. Ninety-six passengers died of typhoid during the voyage. When the *Ticonderoga* arrived in Port Phillip, it flew a yellow flag to signal there was disease on board.

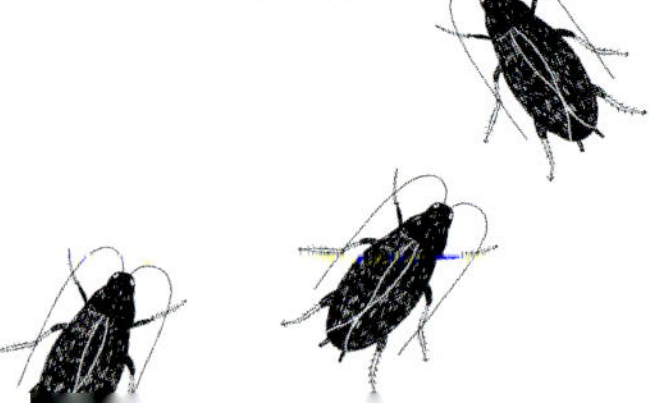

Determined to keep typhoid out of Melbourne, the Victorian Government assigned funds for a quarantine station at Point Nepean.
The superintendent of the quarantine station said the spread of typhoid was the result of 'a bad captain, an inefficient doctor and a dirty ship'.

It wasn't until 1880 that doctors discovered that a bacteria caused typhoid and that it was transmitted by infected food and water. A vaccine to combat typhoid was developed in 1896.

Over the Seas to a New Life

People continued to sail across Bass Strait from Van Diemen's Land to settle in Melbourne. In 1839, 200 migrants from overseas arrived via Sydney on the *Hope*. Later that year the *David Clark* brought the first immigrants directly from Britain to Melbourne. The passengers were unloaded at Sandridge, now called Port Melbourne. Sailors carried women and children ashore on their backs. The new arrivals then had to walk 3 kilometres to their new homes – tents.

These migrants were the first to come to Melbourne on the 'Bounty Scheme'. The government paid shipowners a bounty to bring British workers to the colony. Between 1839 and 1850, an average of one immigrant ship per week arrived in Melbourne, bringing a total of 25,000 assisted migrants. Almost a quarter of them were children. By 1850, 35 per cent of Melbourne's population was assisted migrants.

1839–1869

One of the most famous immigrant ships was the *Great Britain*. Built in 1843, it was the largest passenger ship at that time. It was also the first built of iron to have a screw propellor. This enabled the *Great Britain* to complete the journey from Liverpool, England, to Melbourne in 61 days. The *Great Britain* made 32 voyages to Australia in 24 years. This one ship brought a total of 20,000 migrants to Australia.

Many Irish people emigrated to Australia because of widespread famine in their country. The famine had resulted in more than a million people dying of hunger. Those who could afford to leave Ireland sailed to Australia or America, hoping for a better life. One immigration scheme shipped more than 4000 orphan girls from Ireland between 1849 and 1851. Of those, 1700 arrived in Melbourne.

Rush for Gold

In 1851, with much celebration, Melbourne separated from New South Wales to become an independent colony. The new colony was named Victoria after the reigning queen in Great Britain. A few months later, the announcement of large finds of gold near Ballarat and Bendigo sparked Victoria's gold rush. Many workers left their jobs to try their luck at making a fortune on the goldfields.

The ship *Nelson* had left London before news of the Victorian gold rush reached England. When it arrived in Port Phillip, the crew and passengers were surprised to see at least 50 deserted ships anchored in Hobsons Bay. The ships' crews had all left for the goldfields. The crew of the *Nelson* soon joined them and headed for the goldfields. The *Nelson* lay at anchor for more than four months. Eventually, the captain managed to gather a new crew and prepared to return to London. The ship was loaded with a cargo of wool and 227 grams of gold worth more than $45,000.

On the night of 1 April 1852, the captain went ashore but didn't post a guard. He left the ship and its cargo in the charge of the chief officer and seven crew members. At 2 am, two boats rowed up to the

1852–late 1860s

Nelson carrying about twenty men. They silently boarded the ship and overpowered the sleeping crew, tying them up with strips of tablecloth. The robbers knew what they were looking for and soon located the gold.

The police tracked down some of the thieves, arrested them, and charged them with the robbery. They received long sentences of hard labour in chains building Victoria's roads. The police recovered only $4000 worth of gold. The rest was never found.

News of the Victorian gold rush spread. Hundreds of ships arrived in Port Phillip. With the promise of earning as much on the goldfields in a day as they could working on a ship for a year, more and more sailors deserted their ships. Melbourne's ports were soon crowded with empty ships.

During the 1850s, more than a third of the world's gold production came from the Victorian goldfields. Melbourne became one of the richest cities in the world.

1869–1880s From Sail

Sailing ships only needed wind to sail – but they relied on the wind blowing in the right direction to get them to their destination. If the wind was blowing the wrong way, sailors had to use manoeuvres such as tacking, which involved zig-zagging into the wind.

Early sailing ships travelling to Australia took the shortest route from Cape Town, on the tip of Africa, across the Indian Ocean. When there was no wind, the ships were becalmed or stuck in 'the doldrums'. Sailors and passengers suffered long periods in hot weather without a breath of wind.

The clipper ship *Thermopylae* made its first journey from England to Australia in a record-breaking 63 days, arriving in Melbourne on 9 January 1869. Melburnians could hardly believe it was the same ship that had left London on 5 November the previous year. But when it was confirmed, crowds of people went to Port Melbourne to see the handsome sailing ship.

Ships' captains didn't want to return to Britain with an empty ship, so they needed a cargo that would sell in Britain. After the ships left Australia, they often sailed to China to collect a cargo of tea, which became a popular drink in Britain. By the 1880s, Melbourne had become the main exporter of Australian wool.

to Steam

The *Thermopylae* became a wool clipper, carrying more than 4000 bales of wool on each voyage. Clipper ships raced each other, not wanting to miss the wool auctions in London at the beginning of each year. The first captain to arrive was treated like a celebrity.

Auxiliary steamers used a combination of sail and steam in the 1850s but couldn't make the journey by steam alone. Powered by burning coal, steamships needed to visit ports along the way to take on coal. It wasn't until near the end of the 19th century that steamships replaced sailing ships. Sailors no longer needed to scramble up masts to set sails. Instead, they stoked huge coal fires below decks in the engine room.

Clipper ships sailed the seas from the 1840s to 1890s. Built for speed, clippers were streamlined sailing ships, with a long narrow hull, a sharply pointed bow, up to six masts and as many square sails as they could fit. They sailed the Great Circle Route, which took a loop much further south until the ship caught strong and reliable winds known as the 'Roaring 40s'. This route made the trip quicker, sometimes halving the length of the voyage. But the Great Circle had its own dangers. Ships sailed close to Antarctica and risked colliding with icebergs.

Fears and Scares 1864–1890s

Thanks to the gold rush, Melbourne's banks were bursting with millions of dollars in gold and coins – and the whole world knew it! Australian ports also had large stores of coal to fuel steamships.

When Russian naval ships started cruising the Pacific Ocean, the Victorian Government became nervous. In 1864, *The Times* of London warned of a Russian invasion. The following year, a warship with cannons jutting out of its portholes sailed into Port Phillip. It was not a Russian ship, but American.

The American Civil War was raging. The *Shenandoah* was a Confederate ship known to have destroyed six United States vessels. Her captain had come to Melbourne asking for help to repair his ship. He also needed coal and supplies.

Permission was granted, and three weeks later the *Shenandoah* sailed out of Port Phillip. As well as coal, below decks there were also 40 Melbourne men who had secretly signed up as crew.

The *Shenandoah* sank at least 25 more United States vessels. Although the Confederate ship had not been a threat to Melbourne, it had shown how easily an armed ship could enter the bay. Melbourne urgently needed better defences.

Forts and gun batteries built earlier around Port Phillip were in disrepair. New fortifications were proposed, but it was twenty years before they were completed.

Fort Gellibrand was built on the shores of the Williamstown Peninsula. Point Nepean – on the tip of Mornington Peninsula – protected the eastern side. Inside the bay, minefields were laid and three more forts were built – Swan Island Fort, South Channel Fort and Fort Franklin.

Fort Queenscliff defended the western side of The Heads and was the headquarters of this chain of forts. By the 1890s, Melbourne was one of the best-defended harbours in the British Empire.

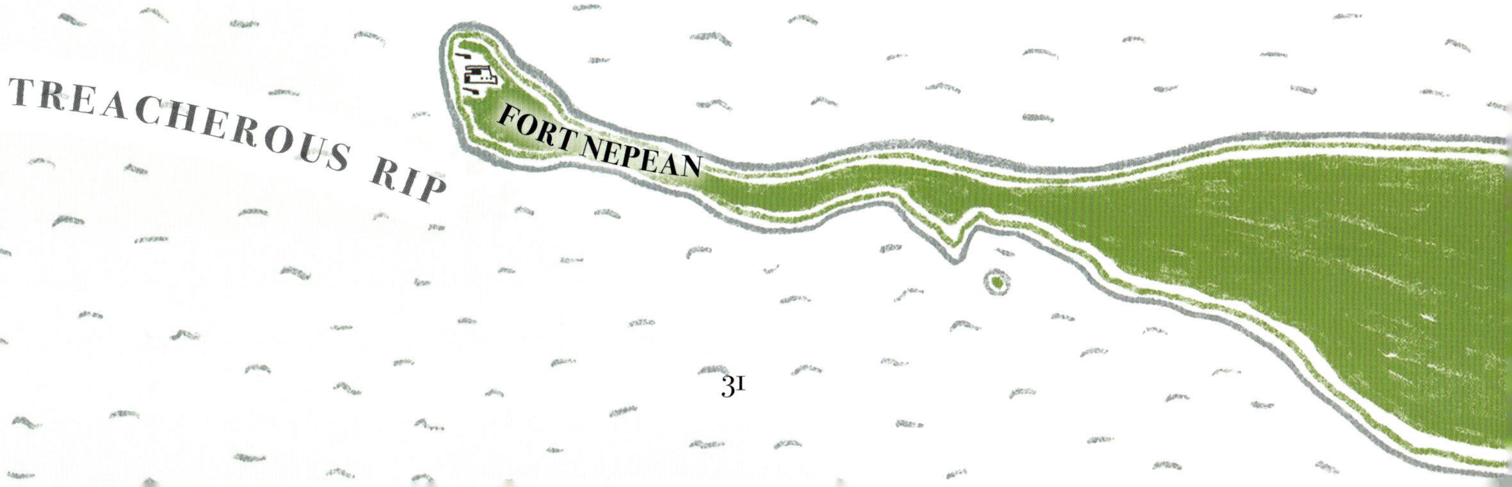

Changing the Course of the Yarra 1879–1892

By the 1870s, Melbourne was no longer the farming community Batman and Fawkner had envisaged. It was called 'Marvellous Melbourne' and had become a city, with many magnificent buildings and ports busy with ships from around the world. And ships were getting bigger.

The Yarra River, however, hadn't changed. It was still a shallow, winding watercourse. It was difficult for ships to navigate the river, particularly around Fishermans Bend. Larger ships had to anchor in Port Phillip. Their cargo and passengers were then ferried up the river on smaller craft – for a price. A plan was needed to allow larger ships to sail all the way to Melbourne.

The government hired Sir John Coode, a British engineer who had experience in designing harbours around the world. Coode came up with a radical plan. He wanted to change the course of the river, making it deeper and wider.

Work on what became known as the Coode Scheme began in 1880. Unemployed labourers were hired to work on Coode's project. They dug 4 kilometres of new river channel using mainly hand tools, removing the unwanted soil in wheelbarrows.

When the sluice gates holding back the river were opened, it took six days for the new channel to fill. The Yarra from the bay to the edge of the city was now an elegant curve. It was 1.5 kilometres shorter, about 7 metres deeper and 100 metres wider.

Coode also planned three new docks. However, only one was built. Victoria Dock was constructed alongside Spencer Street Railway Station so that cargo could be transferred directly onto trains. The dock was also close to the city and its warehouses.

With an area of 39 hectares, 21 large ships could be berthed at Victoria Dock at once. When the dock opened in 1892, Melburnians could boast that it was the second-largest dock in the world.

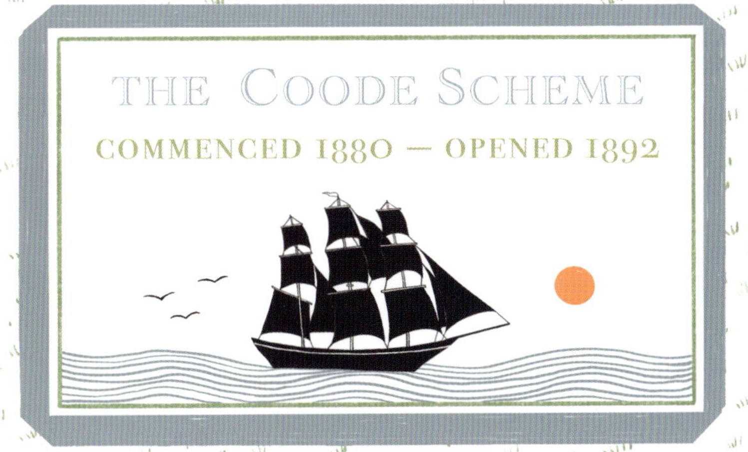

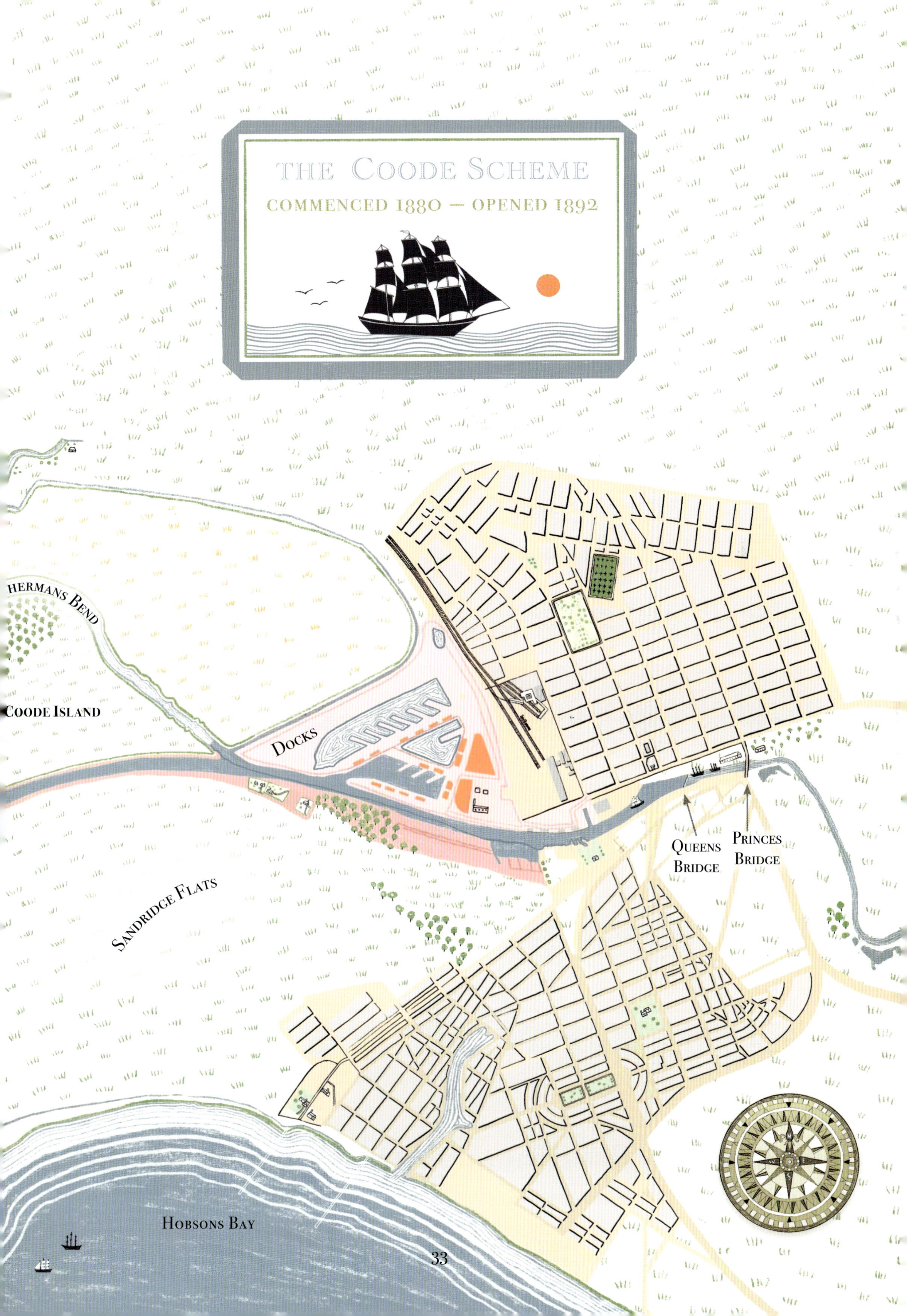
THE COODE SCHEME
COMMENCED 1880 — OPENED 1892
HERMANS BEND
COODE ISLAND
DOCKS
SANDRIDGE FLATS
QUEENS BRIDGE
PRINCES BRIDGE
HOBSONS BAY

Stacked Ships and a Collapsed Bridge

The docks have moved westward and the Port of Melbourne is now closed to the public.

Most cargo is now transported in shipping containers. These steel containers have been used since the early 1950s.

The Port of Melbourne is Australia's largest cargo and container port. It manages about a third of Australia's container shipping. More than 3000 ships visit each year.

1950s – present

A container ship is like a huge barge with containers stacked on its decks. The containers are lifted on and off by massive cranes. A typical container ship can carry thousands of shipping containers.

Not all cargo ships carry containers. Some transport grain, sugar and fertiliser in their holds.

The West Gate Bridge was built to move traffic across the Yarra more efficiently. It has five lanes carrying traffic into the city, and five lanes carrying traffic out. Travellers can get a sense of the size and shape of the Port of Melbourne when driving over the West Gate Bridge.

Construction of the West Gate Bridge began in 1968. Two years later, a 112 metre span between two piers collapsed and fell 50 metres. Thirty-five workers were killed and eighteen injured.
A Royal Commission into the collapse found it occurred when two sections were out of alignment by 11 centimetres.
A decision to weigh down the higher section with ten concrete slabs caused the span to buckle. It remains Australia's worst industrial accident. The bridge was completed safely in 1978.

Keeping the Birrarung Alive 1840s–present

The Woiwurrung and Boonwurrong peoples have retained a close connection to the river.

In the 1840s, two Aboriginal Elders, Billibellary and Bebejan, asked the 'Protector of Aborigines' for land along the Birrarung so they could settle permanently. The Elders' request was denied. In 1863, their sons, Simon Wonga and William Barak, again petitioned the parliament for land. Eventually, the government established Coranderrk Aboriginal Mission, close to the Birrarung, 50 kilometres north-east of Melbourne.

In 1886, laws forced Aboriginal people aged between 15 and 35 with European ancestors to leave Coranderrk. With no young people to work the station, it fell into disrepair and closed in 1924.

The Victorian Government returned Coranderrk cemetery to the Wurundjeri people in 1991. In the following years, the Kulin people were able to take back 119 hectares of Coranderrk. In June 2017, the Yarra River Protection (Wilip-gin Birrarung murron) Bill was introduced into the Victorian Parliament. This was the first time a piece of legislation had its title recorded in an Aboriginal language as well as in English. Wilip-gin Birrarung murron means 'Keep the Birrarung alive' in Woiwurrung.

This was also the first time Wurundjeri Elders – draped in traditional possum-skin cloaks – addressed the Victorian Parliament. In English and Woiwurrung, the Elders explained their connection to Birrarung and the importance of protecting the river for future generations.

Glossary

American Civil War: a war fought between the north and the south of America between 1861 and 1865. The north was known as the Union and the south as the Confederacy or the Confederate States.

assisted migrants: people emigrating from one country to another with financial help from a government.

bow: the front of a ship.

Confederate: a word describing something belonging to the Confederate States of America, e.g. soldiers or ships.

doldrums (the): the name given to an area of ocean just north and south of the Equator where there is often little or no wind and it is hot and humid. In the days of sailing ships, this meant they were often unable to sail, leaving them stranded for days or weeks.

famine: a serious shortage of food when many people die of hunger.

gun batteries: a fortification where an army places large guns to defend land or buildings.

hull: the main body of a ship that keeps it afloat.

Kulin Nation: five Aboriginal communities that are the traditional custodians of land around Port Phillip. They are: Boonwurrung, Dja Dja Wurrung, Taungurung, Wathaurung and Woiwurrung.

legislation: the making of laws.

minefield: an area on land or in the sea where explosive mines (small powerful bombs) have been laid to stop enemies from attacking.

pasture: land covered with grass that is good for livestock such as sheep or cows.

penal colony: a settlement usually in a remote place where criminals are sent for punishment.

quarantine: when people or animals are isolated from others to prevent the spread of disease.

screw propellor: several blades angled to push against the water to propel a ship forward.

sluice gates: barriers that hold back water in rivers or canals until they are opened and allow the water to flow.

typhoid: an infectious, life-threatening disease spread by a bacteria called *Salmonella typhi*, usually through contaminated water or food.

wharf/wharves: a structure along the edge of a harbour where ships can dock so that they can load or unload passengers or cargo.

Index